Bialosky's Big Mystery

Written by
Anne Kostick

Illustrated by
Jerry Joyner

Created by Peggy & Alan Bialosky

One day, Bialosky was getting ready to go out when there was a knock on the door.

A letter fell through the slot.

"I wonder what it could be," said Bialosky.

He decided to open it right away.

"What a mysterious letter," Bialosky
said. "This picture looks like an apple,
and this one looks like a tree. Wait a
minute—there's an apple tree right
down the street."

He put on his detective's hat, and
went out to the apple tree.

There was a picnic basket under the tree. Bialosky lifted the lid.

"This looks like a very important case!" said Bialosky. "Now let's see—this is a chicken, and this is a cage. Mr. Green has a chicken coop near his garden."

Bialosky ran to Mr. Green's chicken coop and looked around.

"I beg your pardon," Bialosky said
to a hen, as he carefully lifted her up.

"I'm solving the mystery!" Bialosky cried. "A sun and a flower—a sunflower!" There are sunflowers right here in Mr. Green's garden."

Bialosky looked under and around each sunflower, but he couldn't find any clues.

Bialosky was baffled. "Maybe I'm in the wrong garden," he said. He walked to the garden gate and opened it.

"Aha!" cried Bialosky. "There goes my clue!"

He chased the van all the way down the street, around the corner, and right to the Sunflower Pet Shop. In the store was a covered bird cage. Pinned to the cover was a big letter B.

"B," he said, "stands for Bialosky. Is
the next clue under the cover?"

"That was a very noisy clue,"
Bialosky said, covering his ears.
"There's a candy store down the street. I
wonder if I'll find another clue there."

In the candy store there was a very
big box of candy.

"Books?" Bialosky said, popping a candy in his mouth. "There are lots of books in the library. That's where I'll go next."

It was almost closing time when he got there, but Mrs. Carr the librarian handed Bialosky a book.

"I'm sure you'll like this one," she
said with a smile. "I've marked a place
in it just for you."

"I know that statue," Bialosky cried. "It's right here in our park!"

Bialosky raced to the park. He searched all over, but there wasn't a letter, or a note, or any clue at all. Bialosky sat down feeling gloomy.

Suddenly he noticed that the statue was pointing to a house he knew. It belonged to his friend Suzie.

There were all Bialosky's friends
and neighbors smiling and laughing.
There was a delicious supper all ready
to eat.

"Did I solve the mystery?" Bialosky
asked.

"Of course," said Suzie. "You found
your own birthday party!"

"Oh, Bumblebees! I forgot all about
my birthday," Bialosky cried.

"Well, don't forget to open your present," said Mrs. Carr.

"Happy Birthday, Bialosky!"
everyone cheered.

"Whew!" said Bialosky, waving his
new magnifying glass. "It's lucky I'm so
good at solving mysteries. Next year on
my birthday, I'll be ready for anything!"